The Horse

C000176292

Written by Lisa Thompson
Pictures by Andy and Inga Hamilton

When Prince Axel woke up, he didn't feel at all normal.

He trotted outside on his hands and knees. He ate some grass.

Prince Axel didn't talk. Instead he neighed like a horse.

5

Princess Daisy Boo made a special grass milkshake. The Prince drank it all.

"That should break the spell," said the Princess.

It did not. Prince Axel ate more grass.

The Princess got her wishing brush.

She brushed her brother's hair while saying a wish.

"Horse be gone
Brother back
Make it quick
With this brush tap."

"That should break the spell," she said.

It did not. Prince Axel bit the wishing brush.

9

The Queen bought four lucky horseshoes.

She put them on Prince Axel's hands and feet.

"That should break the spell," she said.

It did not. Now the Prince clip-clopped around the castle.

11

The Queen washed the Prince with Horse-Away soap.

"That should break the spell," she said.

It did not. Prince Axel ran faster and faster.

The King fed the Prince a magic apple.

"That should break the spell,"
said the King.

It did not. The Prince bit all the apples
and dug up all the carrots.

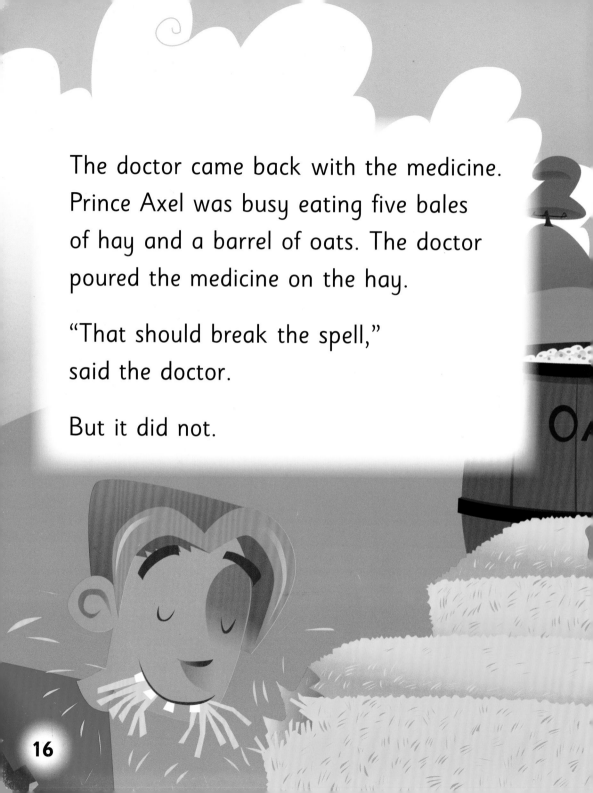

The doctor came back with the medicine. Prince Axel was busy eating five bales of hay and a barrel of oats. The doctor poured the medicine on the hay.

"That should break the spell," said the doctor.

But it did not.

"The Prince will be a horse forever," said the King.

"We shall have to move him into the stables," said the Queen.

"Can I have his room?" asked the Princess. "It's much bigger than mine."

"I can't see why not," said the Queen.

19

The Queen tried one last thing to break the spell. She tapped the Prince's head with her yellow flower.

The Prince let out a huge sneeze.

"Ahhhhhhhchhooooooo!" he cried.

"No, you cannot have my room!" said the Prince.

The spell was broken. Prince Axel was no longer a horse.

But he still eats oats for breakfast. He also loves to crunch on apples and carrots.

How did they
break the spell?

Which idea did you
think was the best one
for breaking the spell?
Why?

Why do you
think the Prince
still eats oats for
breakfast?